THE SELF-TAUGHT FLUTE PLAYER

A GUIDE FOR UNLOCKING FLUTE-PLAYING TECHNIQUES

LOUISE LAWRENCE

Uptake publications

CONTENTS

A Wizwind inspiration

Uptake publications

Taunton. *TA4 2AR*

DEDICATION

With grateful thanks to the Canasta King

INTRODUCTION

How can I make my breath last longer?
Why do some notes sound weaker than others?
How can I improve my coordination?

These commonly asked questions and many more are answered in *The Self Taught Flute Player*.

This neat little guide offers an original, highly effective and succinct visual approach to quickly mastering the correct basics of flute technique. Learning by yourself can feel rather lonely, and without a witness to your progress it is all too easy to pick up habits that will limit your progress.

Keep this friendly book on your music stand as a touchstone for all practice sessions and dip into it when you pause for breath.

Rather than replicate the many comprehensive tutor books and online videos already available, this book focuses on the most common issues you are likely to come across along the way. Hopefully you will find the advice contained within these pages interesting and fun.

Why the pictures? Because we all learn differently. An idea put one way can be baffling, put another can be obvious. I'm a visual learner. If an idea is given to me in picture form, I get it immediately and the message endures. Hopefully, my quirky illustrations will act as a trigger, reminding you of the points taught in the text, whether a guinea pig, a soft-boiled egg or a puppet.

This is the rough order of things:

- **Nuts and bolts of the Flute itself: How best to set it up**
- **How to get the best sound: control of mouth, body, breath and tongue**
- **How to manage the instrument: control of fingers and harnessing the brain**
- **Accessories, trouble shooting and maintenance**

....oh yes and

Back page – *at the back of the book! BUT you may want to read this page first....*

Happy playing!

INSTRUMENT PURCHASE

A BIT OF SAVVY AVOIDS DISAPPOINTMENT

Instrument Purchase – some thoughts:

It really *is* advisable to buy from a music shop specialising in woodwind instruments. Why? Because instruments usually come from the factory needing final preparation before re-sale – a job the shop's repairer will do

Your instrument will come with a warranty, and the shop's repairer will sort out technical issues. Non-specialist shops often send instruments away to get the job done – which means involving a third party and a frustrating wait for you.

There are plenty of sparkly new instruments available online, but best to be a bit savvy.

Some manufacturers cut corners in construction and/or use inferior quality materials – this will ultimately affect your progress. My instrument technician friends now refuse to work on cheap quality imports because they cannot be made to play well.

Second-hand instruments can be economic and successful if you can get your purchase to a teacher or repairer first. Let them check it through for you before you commit to payment.

The best scenario is you could find a real gem; the worst is you could buy an instrument needing extensive overhaul or repair before it plays as it should. If you go the second-hand route, it's wisest and best to take advice.

PUTTING THE FLUTE TOGETHER

THE SAFE WAY

This might seem straightforward with only three sections, but it's important to align these correctly to maximise tone production and minimise strain in the right hand. How you position the joints in relation to each other will affect your posture.

Cup your left hand around the flute body (the longest section), just above the G sharp key. Be aware – it is easy to bend this key.

Holding the foot-joint (shortest section) in your right hand with thumb across the two lower metal cups, twist so the rod is aligned half-way across the lowest metal cup of the middle joint. Imagine a line drawn across this metal cup.

Watch out for the G sharp key

Aligning the foot joint

Now take the head-joint in your right hand – just below the lip plate. Twist it around so the hole is in line with the small top cup at the front of the flute. On some makes of flute you may find a small line engraved on the body of the flute and on the head-joint to enable you to align correctly.

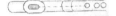

Aligning the head joint

If the head joint is turned in too far toward you, this can dull your sound and make you play flat. Turning the head joint out too far will induce you to raise your left elbow and put a strain on the upper arm.

3

EMBOUCHURE

DRAWER JAW

Understanding how it works

Blowing across the embouchure hole creates a stream of air. This stream of air hits the back of the hole and splits. This is what creates the sound. If you can channel all the air to the back of the hole without wastage, your sound will be clear and focussed.

Before you try to make a sound on the head joint, it may be useful to try the following steps:

1. How does it feel – head joint on the jaw

Place your right-hand index finger in the natural groove just under your lower lip and chin. The flute head joint will sit here.

2. How does it feel – lips against the embouchure hole

Make the sound of a letter *'Pe'…..'pe – pe – pe'*. Notice how the lips and corners of the mouth are relaxed. Now try the same shape with *'Whe'……'whe – whe – whe'* – keep the lips and corners of mouth relaxed as with the per sound. Now try a sustained jet of air with the *whe* shape – '*whe*_____'

NB – By contrast

'**Whoo**' pulls the corners of the mouth inwards and bunches the lips forward into a kissing shape.

'**Whee**' pulls the corners of the mouth out and pulls the lips straight like a taught washing line.

Neither of these shapes will work for you.

Go back to '*whe* – *whe* – *whe*', then '*whe*——————'.

Keep a check on how this feels.

3. How does it feel – jaw (the drawer)

Now hold your right hand in front of your face, palm inwards. Create your '*whe*—— ' with a steady stream of air. Feel the jet of air on your palm.

Move that jet of air up and down. Be sure to keep your head absolutely still, do not move the head up and down. Imagine whistling a high note and then a low note. Notice that your jaw moves *forward* to direct the air *upwards* and *back* to direct the air *downwards*. Your jaw moves in and out like a drawer.

Drawer-jaw

Now you are ready to work with the head joint. Try this in front of the mirror:

Place the head joint on the groove just under your bottom lip with the open end facing to your right. Cover the open end with the palm of your right hand. Move the head joint so that the hole is central on your lip. With your left hand, roll the flute backwards and forward slightly.

If you *can't see any* of the hole, then you are **turned in too far**.

If you **can see all** of the hole, then you are turned **out too far**.

You should be able to see just a *semi-circle of open hole*.

Position of embouchure hole

Now try the *'whe————'* stream of air. Experiment with tiny adjustments of the jaw-drawer movement, forwards and back, correcting very slightly until you can get a good bodied sound – most note, least air.

Check in the mirror that the head joint is in the middle of your lip and that you can only see a semi-circle of hole.

NB: it is possible to get a strong sound by turning the flute inwards, but this has the effect of dulling the note and pitching too low.

4

___

POSTURE
TREE ROOTS

Think about this

Breathing needs to be free and unrestricted. Fingers need to be loose and flexible. Aside from discomfort arising from repetitive strain, tensions in neck, shoulder, upper back and arms can inhibit breathing and swift movement of the fingers, so how you position your body in relation to the Flute is very important.

This needs particular consideration because the overall positioning is not symmetrical.

Lower body - check

Keep your feet comfortably straight and planted slightly apart. Place your left foot slightly forward from the right. The weight of the body is now supported predominantly by the left foot rather than the right.

This posture will ensure that you are correctly inline and balanced as you play and that your torso is not twisted. Allow a slight softness and flexibility in the knees. The knees act in a similar way to the suspension on a car, absorbing any undesired body movement so that it will not impact on the rest of the body.

Softness in knees for suspension

If you are securely attached to the floor, you will feel more in control of yourself and your instrument. You will be less likely to suffer from nerves or anxiety and will look more professional. Whatever situation you may be playing in, you will feel relaxed and flexible yet firm and grounded.

Flexible and grounded - like a rooted tree

Upper body - check

Place all your fingers into position on the flute and raise the instrument to your lips as if you were about to play.

Right arm – right hand

With little finger on the E^b key and the thumb underneath the index finger, the elbow should drop down comfortably, neither tucked into the body, or held out like a wing – about 45 degree angle should feel comfortable.

Left arm – left hand

As with the right elbow, the left elbow drops down comfortably, neither tucked into the body, or held out like a wing – again, about 45 degree angle should feel comfortable.

Chin

This should be slightly raised, as if seeing over the head of a tall person sitting in the cinema seat in front of you.

Head

This should be very slightly cocked to the right, as if asking someone a question.

Tilting the head slightly to the right

Mirror

If you check this stance in front of a mirror, you will see the end of the flute is angled slightly lower on the right than the left. There is also plenty of gap between the left shoulder and the head joint. Enough to seat a healthy-sized guinea pig.

Enough room on the shoulder to seat a healthy-sized guinea pig

Embouchure

Check your embouchure position has not changed and the Flute is still central on your lower lip.

Sitting down

Three things to consider when you are sitting down to play:

1. Upper posture is exactly the same as when you stand

2. Position yourself sideways on to the music so that the body is in line with the flute and the torso is not twisted.

3. Sit towards the front edge of the chair so you optimise the length of the upper body.

Sitting towards the back of the chair induces slouching, and this impacts on breathing capacity and flexibility of posture. Sitting upright also increases alertness and concentration.

Edge of chair posture for breathing and alertness

5

POSITION OF HANDS AND FINGERS

TWO ANCHOR POINTS

Pick up your flute and consider the following:

Left hand

Curve the index finger of your left hand and thumb into the shape of a letter C. Notice the fleshy area between the two knuckles of the index finger – the one at the base of the finger, and the next knuckle up where the index finger bends.

Left index finger curve

Nestle the flute on this cushion of flesh, and then twist your wrist outwards very slightly so that the side of the index finger is pushing the head joint against your chin.

With the fingers placed on the keys, thumb on either the B natural or B flat thumb key, check the pressure of the fingers on the keys is gentle but firm, not pressing hard, hand relaxed and rounded as if enclosing a warm soft-boiled egg.

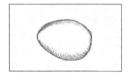

Hands relaxed and rounded as if enclosing a warm soft-boiled egg

Right hand

With the fingers placed on the keys, (little finger on Eb key), move your right-hand thumb so it is underneath the right-hand index finger. When holding this position, be gently firm, but do not press hard, hand relaxed and rounded, imagine holding that warm soft-boiled egg.

Anchoring between only two points

Think about this

The only two places on the flute that never lose contact with the fingers are *the side of the left hand index finger,* and *the thumb of the right hand.* Therefore, for absolute control, these are the only two points you can rely on as anchoring points.

Try this

See if you can slide the right-hand thumb from under the flute ever so slightly towards you and around the tube. Notice, instead of the flute resting on the thumb, the thumb is now pushing against the side of the tube. The flute is being pushed by the right thumb against the side of the left index finger.

If you have these two anchor points correctly placed, the flute will be perfectly balanced. To test this out, take the tip of the left index finger off the B key and the left thumb off its key. Now take the right little finger off the E flat key. Ensure that you are keeping the fingers still very close to the flute. Movement should be no more than a fraction of a centimetre. If you are accustomed to playing with your right thumb under the flute, this may feel awkward and unnatural at first. The flute is likely to roll towards you because the weight of the key work is on the side of the flute nearest your body.

Just experiment with tiny adjustments, sliding the flute head joint up the left index finger, the right thumb further up around the tube, and turning the flute out slightly until it is balanced perfectly, with no roll.

If you can achieve this, swift movements between the open notes and the upper register should be more easily controlled, and repetitive strain in the right hand should be minimised. Players of open holed flutes with in-line G will also appreciate that the finger pads are now seated correctly over the keys.

Anchor points for security

NB

Physiology varies. Hand size and finger length may have a bearing on comfort and management of technique. It's a question of understanding the logic, trying suggestions and then working with what is manageable for you

6

DIAPHRAGM BREATHING

PUPPETS AND BALLOONS

Make the most of your air. The diaphragm muscle is a like a large elasticated rubber sheet situated between the lungs and the stomach. Used well, you can use it to take in more air and control how you let the air out.

How does it feel?

Imagine blowing out candles on a birthday cake (cheeks slightly puffed). Prepare yourself for this - there are 100 candles!

Birthday cake blowing is shallow

Notice how the shoulders rise and the stomach is pulled in?

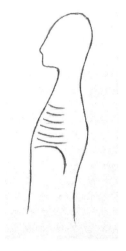

Less air is taken in

Blow the birthday cake air out onto the palm of your hand, and it will feel cold because the air has been sucked only part way into the lungs. The only way to control the speed and strength of that jet of air is by pursing the lips into a whistling shape. This shallow breathing is not making best use of the diaphragm. Notice also how extra tension is stored in the upper body, shoulders and arms? This will adversely affect posture and flexibility of finger technique.

Now imagine breathing steam on a window pane. Prepare yourself for this - it is a full length french window!

Steamy window breathing is deeper

Notice how this time the shoulders stay relaxed and the abdomen extends?

More air is taken in

Breathe the window air onto the palm of your hand and it will feel warm because you have taken air right down to the bottom of your lungs. You can breathe your lungful of air out slowly and steadily, or more quickly in a fast 'Ha'. This deeper breathing is making good use of the diaphragm. Upper body, shoulders and arms are now relaxed. This will improve posture and flexibility of finger technique.

Exercises to get started

NB: *These exercise are best managed in front of a good sized mirror so you can keep a check on what is happening.*

First of all, we need to get a sense of where the diaphragm is. To do this, just place a hand on your stomach - somewhere between the bottom of your rib cage and your belly button. Make three short sniffs in close succession. You will feel your stomach puff up like a balloon.

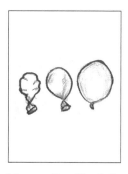

Abdomen puffs up like a balloon

If you stand side end on to your mirror when you do this, you will see your abdomen extend.

Turn back to face the mirror.

To make best use of the diaphragm, the shoulders should stay in a relaxed position and never become raised.

Imagine you are a puppet. The strings holding up your arms have been cut so that your arms are hanging loose and relaxed by your sides.

Arms floppy and relaxed - like a puppet with no strings

Place your hand back on your stomach and make those three sniffs again - stomach puffing up like a balloon.

Relax, and let the air out. Repeat this exercise a few times.

Now try continuing on to five or six sniffs until your stomach feels fully extended - air sucked down to the bottom of the lungs. Relax and let the air out. Repeat a few times. Keep a check in the mirror - shoulders should not rise, arms floppy and relaxed.

When this feels natural, open your mouth very slightly and:

LET the air *in* - one long swoop (abdomen extends out).

LET the air *out* (abdomen relaxes back).

Check in the mirror that the shoulders are not raising up. If they are, go back to the puppet position, arms floppy and relaxed by your sides. Then try the exercise again.

(Just an aside here – the word 'let' is more useful than 'breathe' in this exercise. The word 'breathe' usually triggers automatic reverting to default breathing habits. Interestingly, if you were to lie on the floor you would find your stomach fills out when you breathe in, and relaxes as you breathe out).

Now pick up the flute and take a long swoop of air into the diaphragm, and breathe out through the flute on a bottom E.

Check in the mirror. Your shoulders should not move.

Test it out

Check how long your bottom E note lasts. You can practise your breathing technique anywhere any time. The more you exercise the diaphragm, the longer your bottom E will become, and the more control you will have over your flute sound.

Think about this

Learning to use your diaphragm when you breathe will not only hugely benefit your flute playing. Diaphragm breathing also reduces the effects of anxiety – a wonderful skill that can be used in your every-day life!

Caution:

If you feel light-headed, just take a break and come to the exercise later.

7

CONTROLLING THE TONE

TUBES OF SOUND

The quality of the sound you produce comes down to two things:

1. Developing the concept of a good tone in your head.

2. Developing control of the lip and diaphragm muscles.

The concept of a good tone can be developed by plenty of listening. There are so many excellent players out there, and the more you develop your listening experience, the more aware you will become of the sound you would like to produce. When you are working on tone-exercises, unconsciously you will be making tiny adjustments to match the tone you have stored in your head. This is innate – after all, it is through listening and imitation we learn how to speak.

So then it's a matter of developing and controlling your own sound. The very best way to improve your tone is to spend time playing long notes.

Choose a favourite low note. Take in air using your diaphragm. Breathe out through your flute to produce a long steady note. Visualise this as a solid tube of sound. Keep it level – no wavering.

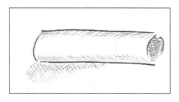

Long steady notes like tubes of sound

Choose a higher note and repeat. Choose a lower note and repeat.

Next, start on a one finger B – lower register. Keep the note level and make it last as long as your breath will allow. As you come to the end of the note, you will feel a tightness in your abdomen. This is your diaphragm pushing out the last dregs of air.

Next, take the air fully into the diaphragm again and play the B, but slur swiftly on down to B^b holding this 2nd note as long as your breath will allow. Take the air into the diaphragm and, starting on the B^b, slur on down to the A, all the while trying to match the sound of the note pairs. Keep working down to bottom C, or B if you have a B foot.

Matching pairs of notes - making your air last

Now start on the B again, and work upwards in a similar fashion, slurring to C, and then from C to C$^{\sharp}$ and onwards up in semi-tones towards the B, an octave higher.

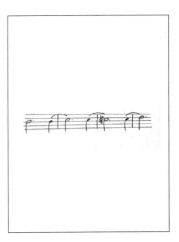

Matching pairs of notes upwards through the open notes

Matching pairs between B, C, C$^{\#}$ and D is also good for matching the tone on the open notes (see Chapter 8).

The more time you spend on long notes, the better your sound will be.

If you do this daily, you may think your note tubes are wavering more than before. Don't be disheartened. You are only becoming more aware and perceptive, which is the surest way to success.

You cannot help but improve by spending time on this activity.

Think about this

Learning to use your diaphragm when you breathe will not only hugely benefit your flute playing. Diaphragm breathing also reduces the effects of anxiety – a wonderful skill that can be used in your every-day life!

NB Listening to the pure tonal quality of each individual note is the purpose of the exercise here, so to get the value from this work, do not be tempted to use vibrato.

8

OPEN NOTES

BALANCING THE TONE

Controlling the open notes

You may notice that C and C[#] on the Flute can have a weaker and less focussed tonal quality in relation to other notes. C and C# are called 'open-notes' and are more difficult to control because so many of the notes are uncovered. These notes also have a tendency to play sharp. This is particularly noticeable when moving between C and D (from few holes covered, to many holes covered). Weakness in tonal quality is also most noticeable when playing long sustained sounds on just C or C#. The following exercise using harmonics can really help with this:

Finger a very bottom C (all fingers on). While playing a long sustained tube of sound, push your jaw forward very slightly until you hear the note move from a low sounding C to a higher sounding C. This is the harmonic C. If you can maintain this jaw position and keep up the air pressure you will be able to hold this higher pitched note. Listen to the quality and pitch of this sound.

Now finger C with the customary fingering (left index and E♭ key). Hold the note whilst listening carefully to the tuning and sound quality. Move backwards and forwards between the harmonic C and the open C fingering. (NB - the notation for harmonic notes is a small circle placed above the note to be fingered).

Matching the harmonic C with open C

Try to match the tonal quality and tuning on the open C, to that of the harmonic C. The sounds will begin to match up because, unconsciously, you will be making slight adjustments to lips, jaw and the oral cavity whilst you are playing – tapping into your innate ability of adjusting your physiology to create the sound you want to emulate.

This exercise can be repeated for C sharp. Create the harmonic C sharp on the low C sharp fingering and balance it out with the open C sharp fingering.

This exercise is also useful for tonal control and tuning throughout the range of the flute. (More on this in chapter 10).

9

TONGUING

THE TINY HAMMER

Tonguing is the technique of separating one note from the next with the tongue. A correct tonguing technique will produce a clear beginning to each note and allow you to play swiftly and neatly. Tonguing on the flute is more straightforward than on clarinet or saxophone, but it's good to be aware of how the tongue moves in the mouth to produce different sounds, so you can be sure you are developing the correct technique.

The way we use the tongue when producing words is instinctive and automatic, but the movements are surprisingly subtle.

Try this in front of a mirror (Whisper, no vocal chords):

'*OO-OO-OO*' (throat opens and closes)

'*Thoo-thoo-thoo*' (tongue flicks between teeth)

'*Doo-Doo-Doo*' (area just behind the tip of the tongue touches roof of mouth with a slightly heavier action).

'Too-Too-Too' (tip of tongue touches roof of mouth lightly with a slightly forward motion)

The '*Too*' action is the one we will be using – there are six important things to notice:

1. The tongue acts like a tiny hammer hitting the roof of the mouth.

2. The tongue movement is soft and gentle yet precise.

3. The movement is slightly forward.

4. The tongue never appears between the lips – it remains invisible.

5. There is no tension in the throat, all the action is in the tongue.

6. Air flow continues through the flute in a solid stream - no faltering.

Now try this:

Get a solid tube of sound going on a nice easy note. Now bring in the *'Too'* action. Notice how every time the tongue hits the roof of the mouth, it stops the air-flow for a split second. The tongue acts like a tiny hammer, hitting the roof of the mouth and separating the notes, chopping up that tube of sound.

The tongue acts like a tiny hammer

Continue with your *'too-too-too'* sounds. Notice also how the air pressure builds behind the tongue, ready to produce the first *'too'* note.

It is important the tongue action remains soft and gentle, so the note can continue between strikes, unimpeded by too much heavy tongue. Imagine a taut washing line (your note tube) with tiny pegs (your tongue strikes). The peg takes up a minute section of space on the line, and it is so small and light that the line continues with minimal interruption

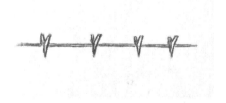

Note continues between tiny tongue strikes - like a washing line between tiny pegs

10

UPPER REGISTER

HOW DOES IT WORK

Remember how the stream of air splits when it hits the back of the embouchure hole? We are now going to change the angle that the air hits the back of the hole. The air is angled upwards to achieve the upper register, so before trying these notes revise the palm blowing exercise (Chapter 3) to reacquaint yourself with the 'jaw-drawer' action needed to move the airstream up the palm.

Play a bottom E, a long-sustained tube of sound, remembering to support from the diaphragm. Now edge the lower jaw forward, (drawer action), until you produce the E an octave higher, and hold this note.

Repeat this with a low F, then G. Once these notes feel secure and you are able to sustain the upper pitch, you can work on upwards to top C or even C$^{\#}$.

It really helps if you can internally pitch your higher notes before playing them, because this brings about the involuntary subtle changes to the mouth cavity that are needed to help you create the sound you are aiming for. You can test this out by singing a low note and then a high note in your head and noticing how this feels.

Here are three visual concepts that have helped pupils to pitch higher notes. One of these might work for you:

Imagine you are blowing a fly off your nose.

Blowing a fly off the nose

Imagine you are presenting a precious tiny pearl seated upon your lower lip.

Presenting a tiny pearl
seated on lower lip

Imagine you are blowing your fringe out of your eyes.

Blowing fringe out of eyes

You can revisit the tone exercise from Chapter 7, but this time start on the upper register B and work down in semitones. All the time, support from the diaphragm, visualise solid tubes of sound – no wavering.

Matching pairs of notes in the upper register

11

STRENGTHENING THE LOWER REGISTER

VIBRANT TUBES OF SOUND

Think about this

Balancing the tone between the lower and the higher registers on the flute is important to gain an overall homogenous effect. Developing resonance in the lower register needs particular attention because it is weaker and has less carrying power than the higher registers. This can be overcome by adding in some harmonic colour.

Try this

Play a low E – level tube of sound, support from the diaphragm. Push forward slightly with the 'jaw-drawer' movement, until you begin to hear the upper E. There is a tipping point between the low E and the E an octave above. Find the point where you are pitching and hearing predominantly a low E, but you begin to hear some 'edge' to the sound – you are introducing some harmonic to your sound. Your previously weak bottom E will now have some colour and depth, and the added bonus of greater carrying power.

Try this on all the notes in the lower register in turn, listening and adapting the jaw movement for optimum effect.

You can re-visit the semitone movement exercise in chapter 7. Start with a vibrant B with harmonic colour, a shiny note tube – supporting from the diaphragm.

Resonant tube of sound

As you move down in semitones, try to match the sound of the second note to the first so your bottom C is as vibrant as the first note B that you started on.

An extra little tip

Try pushing the flute ever so slightly harder into the lower lip. Doing this has the effect of marginally re-directing the air so that the bottom notes are more focussed.

12

NOTE ENDINGS

CLOUDS

Think about this

Working towards creating a beautiful and resonant tone and a clean tonguing technique is important, but if you want your playing to sound fluid and musical, it is also important to think about the ends of the notes too.

Try this

Sing a few phrases of a slow tune – any tune will do – do this to *'la'* . You don't need words, and you don't need a beautiful voice, this is just a private conversation between you and your flute. Listen carefully to the end of each phrase – notice how your voice tapers off slightly? It doesn't end abruptly. We are going to try and emulate this on the flute:

Play a long note of choice in the lower register – a long silvery tube with harmonic colour. Now try raising the head very slightly without changing the embouchure – lips and jaw position do not move. Notice how the sound gently tapers away? Experiment with this effect slowly at first.

Now, try bringing the bottom lip fractionally closer to the upper lip while raising the head, and you will find that you can taper the note more quickly so the head needs to raise less.

Rather than an abrupt stopping of sound, you are now able to achieve a subtle tapering to the end of your silvery note tubes. Think of the sound floating off on a cloud.

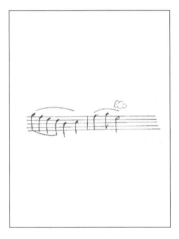

Tapering the ends of notes - like floating on a cloud

When you have mastered this in the lower register, try this exercise in the upper register. This is slightly more difficult to master – you will need to be more aware of diaphragm and embouchure control whilst developing this new technique.

Apply this to your playing, where phrasing allows, and melodies will become lyrical and have a song-like quality.

13

FINGER CO-ORDINATION

SEPARATE THE TASKS

Think about this

The finger co-ordination between certain note pairings can feel awkward and unnatural. The left and right hand need to learn different movements, and particularly when learning top notes, embouchure control is an issue too. This can cause mental overload for some. By separating the tasks, it is possible to embed muscle memory more quickly. To illustrate this learning method, let's work with C and D. The movement between C and D can feel unwieldy and illogical at the outset. There are various reasons for this:

1. Having moved one note at a time, finger by finger upwards from the lower notes of the Flute, the next step from C to D suddenly requires the swift movement of eight fingers simultaneously.

2. The balance of the instrument feels really insecure, moving between two fingers sitting on the flute with *no support from the left-hand thumb,* to five fingers sitting on the flute together *with support* of the left-hand thumb.

3. The tonal quality changes, from a weaker sounding C where many holes are open, to the stronger sounding D where many holes are closed, (see Chapter 8).

4. Remembering to move the little finger so that it is on for C and off for D.

Try this - (breaking down the tasks)

Sit with the end of your flute on your right knee. Clasp your left hand gently around the upper part of the flute. Place your right-hand three fingers down on the keys, the right thumb in position and let the right little finger off the E^b key. Now place the little finger down on the E^b key and let the three fingers come up; now three fingers down and E^b key up. Think of a seesaw. Fingers come up, little finger goes down; little finger comes up, fingers go down. Keep repeating until this feels natural.

Right hand D to C movement

Take your time. Very quickly you will find the brain clicks into place and the movement becomes automatic. Motor-memory.

Now, clasp your right hand gently around the lower part of the flute. Place the fingers and thumb of the left hand down on their keys. Let the index finger of the left hand come up. Now, put the left index down and let the remaining two fingers and thumb come off their keys. As the thumb and two fingers come back onto their keys, let the left index go up – repeat over and over, think of that see saw.

Left hand C to D movement

Now, keeping the Flute on your knee, try co-ordinating both hands together.

Finger the D,

Both hands play D

then finger the C.

Both hands play C

Continue alternating the fingers backwards and forwards until the movement becomes automatic.

Keep your fingers firm but close to the instrument and relaxed throughout this exercise, (more on this in Chapter 20).

Now try playing C to D (blowing the notes).

This approach is a really useful technique for overcoming difficulties in co-ordination. It can be applied to any tricky finger movements.

1. Right hand see-saw

2. Left hand see-saw

3. Both hands together

4. Blowing the notes.

Try it with C$^{\#}$ to D, and D to E and E to F$^{\#}$. All these movements can be challenging early on. Later, when your playing progresses, you can use it for moving from the middle to upper registers.

With these upper notes, you will be multi-tasking even more because you will be thinking about maintaining air-flow and embouchure adjustment whilst working out the co-ordination needed for all the new cross-fingerings.

Break the tasks up and master them each by turn. See-saw for finger co-ordination first - then bring in blowing the notes.

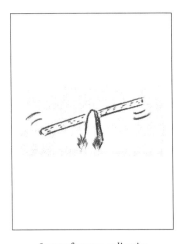

Seesaw finger co-ordination

14

B FLAT FINGERINGS

MAPPING IT OUT

Plan ahead – when to switch and when to use the side key.

If you are working with a flute tutor book, you will have discovered that there are three ways to play B^b. If there is a B^b in the key-signature and the entire piece of music will be using a B^b, then you can just keep the thumb on the B^b thumb key.

If the music switches between B^b and B natural, then you may need to switch your thumb from B^b to B natural.

Let's work with just the thumb keys for now, B^b and B natural. We can look at the alternatives later.

It is a good idea to plan out your thumb movements in advance. If you don't do this (and we can all fall foul of laziness), you are likely to embed repeated mistakes (see motor-memory, Chapter 15).

Try this

Thumb B♭

Asterisk the music at the beginning of the piece with whichever B you are starting with. Move on to where there is a change. Seek out an opportunity to move your thumb *before* the change – this will be either when you are playing a C or C$^{\#}$ because you are not using your thumb, or during a rest when you have time. Asterisk the music with the change of fingering. Continue on in this way, marking out where you need to switch.

Mark thumb key switches with an asterix

Side key B^b

There are times when you will have to move between B^b and B natural quickly and there are no opportunities to switch the thumb. This is where it may be easier to keep the thumb on the B natural key throughout and just use the side-key for passages with B^b. You don't need to asterisk, just bracket the section where you hold the side key down and mark it 'sk'.

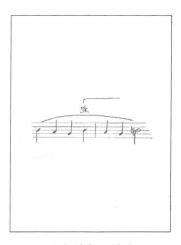

Mark side key with sk

1/1 B♭

If you have your thumb on B natural and you have to move to B♭ from an E or an F, you can use the 1/1 fingering, in which case you can just pop 1/1 above the B♭ and not change the thumb.

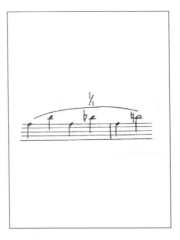

Mark 1 and 1 fingering with 1/1

When you first start a piece, you may need to try different B♭ options. Find the ones that work best, then map out your piece, marking the fingerings and changes. That way, you will be playing all the accidentals correctly from the outset.

Here's a thought – *if you can avoid embedding mistakes at the outset, then you will be making best use of your practice time and progress will be quicker.*

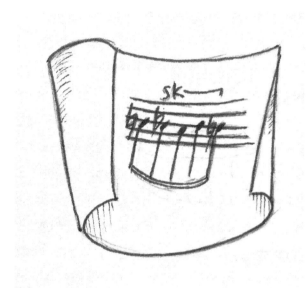

Map out your Bb accidentals

15

SCALES
WHY BOTHER

Why play Scales?

Because scales are the quickest way to learn all the most common finger moves we use in playing music.

Why don't people like playing them?

Because most people get frustrated. They spend ages playing them over and over to get them right, and then when they come back to them later, they go wrong again.

Why does this happen?

Every time a scale goes wrong, your fingers are learning the wrong pattern. If you play the scale over and over, getting it wrong, then you are training your fingers to play a wrong finger pattern – motor memory.

Playing a scale wrong is therefore actually worse than not playing a scale at all!

Why are wrong notes unsettling to hear?

Hearing a different sound to the one you are expecting can be an uncomfortable experience.

Wrong note!!

Solution

When learning a scale for the first time, play it so... so....slowly that you cannot possibly go wrong. It is best to read it from some kind of notation to start off with. Be sure to read the note and know what the fingering is for that note *before* your fingers move there. It is tempting to let the fingers take off and do their own thing.

If you do play a wrong note, correct it – go back to the beginning of the scale and play only as far as the offending note, but finish on the corrected note this time. *Stop*. Play from the beginning again.

Do this three times and you will have re-trained your fingers so that they get it right next time.

Each stair the same space from the last

When you feel more secure with your scale, be content to play slowly and steadily. Imagine an elderly person plodding upstairs. You can upgrade to a more youthful jog when you are feeling even more confident.

16

HOW TO PLAY TRICKY BITS

HARNESSING THE BRAIN

Memorising is a valuable tool. By looking away from the music, you can really think about what your fingers are doing and train them quickly to do what you want.

Try this

Circle the bit you can't play. If this is a whole line of notes, play slowly and work out which notes are the most difficult to move between. Narrow it down to the most challenging three notes, or maybe even just two. Play these notes very slowly from the music three times. Memorise these notes and play them again while looking at a blank wall.

*Looking at a blank wall rather than the music allows
you to think about what your fingers are doing*

You have now trained your fingers into the right finger pattern. Go back to looking at the music and add in *either* the previous note, *or* the note following, so you now have four notes. Repeat the process with these four notes, playing from the page three times and then from memory three times. Continue the process, adding in notes, one by one.

Messy blips - If you have tried this tactic, but things still sound messy, try this:

Take each pair of notes in the phrase and listen carefully as you move between them. Check your fingers are moving together. If they move up or down at different times, then you will hear an extra note in between. Work out which finger is moving up or down <u>last</u>. Work slowly so that you can make that sluggish finger to move up or down <u>first</u>.

Now play the whole phrase and get a tad angry with the sluggish note. It will come out correctly because you are paying it extra attention and therefore anticipating it in advance.

Repeating wrong notes - If you keep playing a wrong note in the same place, don't keep playing it wrong – you will be working the wrong fingering into your technique. Go slowly enough from the beginning of the phrase to get the offending note correct. Then repeat three times ending on the **correct** note. Remember – motor memory – training fingers to do what you want every time.

Keep a check on the state of your brain

This way of working is rewarding, but very intense, so there will come a point when you'll feel tired and things start to fall apart. Maybe change to a different type of practice, now.

Play through something easy you enjoy, or walk away and do something entirely different. Your brain will still be mulling over the niggly problem. When you come back to it next time, you should find, surprisingly, that the awkward section is a lot easier.

17

PLAYING EVEN NOTES SMOOTHLY

IRONING

Think about this

Playing runs of notes quickly and evenly in scales or pieces can be challenging. This is because the co-ordination required between pairs of notes is rarely equal. Think of an E major scale: E / F$^{\#}$ / G $^{\#}$ / A / B

Rising E Major Scale - finger movement is not consistent

The movement between A and B is the only one requiring a single finger movement. The movement between A and B is therefore likely to be executed more quickly than the movements between the other notes in the run.

Try this

Play the E major run of five notes – slow, steady and slurred. Now try it in a dotted rhythm - dotted quaver/semi-quaver rhythm first – you will find this makes you concentrate harder on the individual notes in the run.

When you can play this in a controlled manner, switch the rhythm round the other way - semi-quaver/dotted quaver. This will make you concentrate even harder than before – a good thing, because you are learning the notes within the run more thoroughly.

When you can play the run in both rhythms equally well, try playing the notes in even quavers. You should find that any unevenness has been ironed out.

Notes in a run ironed out and even

NB

When we depress the $G^\#$ and $D^\#$keys with the little fingers, we are pushing against the springing action that holds the keys in place. You need to be aware of this when slurring from $G^\#$ to A, for example, or $D^\#$ to Eb. As the little finger of each hand is weaker than the fourth finger it is likely to be pushed off slightly earlier, so the two fingers won't be moving together.

Check 'messy blips' in Chapter 16 to rectify this. You may find it useful to re-read this chapter if you really want to nail the neat execution of a tricky phrase.

18

READING MUSIC FLUENTLY

EYE HOPPING

If you listen to a young child learning to read, they hesitate between each word:

The.......cat.....sat.......on.......the.......mat.

Big gaps.

If you listen to an adult reading the same sentence, the words blend together:

Thecatsatonthemat.

No gaps.

Try reading the very first sentence on this page – the one in bold italic. Now read it again, but this time read it out loud. When you say the word 'listen', notice which word your eyes are focussed upon... probably on the word 'young' or 'child'.

This is because we scan ahead with our eyes – and of course reading then becomes fluent. In the same way, *music* will sound more fluent if you can read ahead.

Eye hopping

TIP

Rather than resting your eyes on the longer notes when you play them, use the time to read ahead to the next note. You can use this strategy when you get to a rest or a breathing place or the end of a line.

Consciously make yourself do this, and eventually you will find yourself reading ahead on the shorter notes, too. You'll continue to develop until you find yourself scanning ahead many notes at a time as you play.

19

PRACTICE ROUTINE
WATCH TV

Little and often is best. You are likely to progress more quickly with just a few minutes each day than exhausting yourself with a three-hour session at the weekend.

Have a routine. Playing long notes is the best way to start. Get control of your breathing and embouchure. *Rich tubes of sound.* Next, scales and finger exercises – get control of the fingers. Then tricky sections of pieces (whilst the mind is still fresh). Lastly, whatever you fancy.

Vary the tasks. If you are bored with long notes, just do a couple, then move onto something else. If you struggle with a scale or a tricky bit of music, don't keep going beyond the point of weariness or frustration – move on to playing something for fun.

Always try to bring in something utterly new – try new ways of doing things: new finger exercises and routines, new music.

Keep inspired and fresh - Listen to other players and recordings, keep yourself open to new ideas.

Have specific targets to work towards – a "performance" can be as understated as playing a tune to a friend. Aspirations to improve technique can be as humble as being able to play smoothly from one tricky note to another.

Take a break. If your concentration flags, do something entirely different – watch TV, go for a walk – whatever – and amazingly enough, when you come back later – you may well find the niggle you were struggling with has suddenly become easier.....your brain has been working on it while you were away from the flute altogether!

Take a break - give the brain a rest

20

FINGER PRESSURE
DRUMMING

Think about this

Watch any professional player and their fingers seem hardly to move. The more you move your fingers, the more difficult it will be to execute a nimble, neat and co-ordinated finger technique. Anxiety and concentration can cause tension and this leads to strain in arms and fingers, which will slow down your technique.

Try this

Without blowing, finger a bottom D and run your fingers up a scale to C and back again. Do this a couple of times. Now press harder and do the same. Notice how the fingers become sluggish and the hands feel slightly strained.

Now, without your flute, shake your right arm, then your left arm, and shake your right hand, then your left hand – roll your shoulders around.

Drum the fingers of your right hand on the table, and now the left.

Check your posture, (chapter 4), take some steady breaths using your diaphragm (Chapter 6). Now try a slow slurred scale, listening for even finger movement.

Try the scale faster. Try a more challenging scale. Try a tricky passage. Check - how close are your fingers? Be aware of tensions in shoulders, arms and fingers.

Drumming the fingers on a table to relieve tension

21

TUNING

CEILING TO FLOOR

Knowing how to alter your pitch so that you can play in tune with others is important. Your flute will be designed to play slightly sharp when the headjoint is pushed completely in. Even when playing on your own, it is good to get used to playing at the correct pitch.

When you set your flute up, pull the headjoint out about half a centimetre, making sure the tone hole stays in line with the top key (see Chapter 2).

If you want to check your tuning, you can download an app. You don't need anything complicated and there are plenty available at no cost. If you are going to invest in a metronome, then getting one with a tuner built in is even better.

Tune to an 'A'. Keep the head-joint in position, don't let it roll *inwards* (it will play flat), or *outwards* (it will play sharp). Remember the semi-circle of hole

(Chapter 3). Keep the breath-control level. Pulling the head joint out makes the flute *longer,* so this will make the pitch *lower*, and pushing the head joint in makes the flute *shorter,* so this will make the pitch *higher*.

If the flute is warm, the pitch will be higher than if it is cold, so it is better to tune your flute when it is warmed up. Rather than wait for this to happen gradually as you get playing, there is a quicker way.

Try this

Finger a bottom C, (bottom B on B foot joint) so all the finger pads are closed. Cover the tone hole completely with your mouth, and breath hot air steadily through the Flute.

Maintaining pitch while playing

It is common for the pitch to drop as you progress through a piece. You may not even notice this.

Think about this

As you read from the top of a page and progress down, the head tends to move down with the page.

Try this

Keeping your head still, look at the ceiling and move your eyes from the ceiling down the wall to the floor. Notice how an impressive span of distance can be covered by the eyes without the head moving at all!

Now try looking at a piece of music. Keeping your head still, it is perfectly possible to read from the top to the bottom of a page of music while maintaining your head in the same position.

If you lower your head when you play, the pitch drops. Consider this when you approach your next piece of music. Keep your head in position while you play and you will maintain pitch.

Scan with eyes to control tuning

22

CLEANING

Cleaning the inside

If you buy a new flute, you will usually find a cleaning rod and a couple of cloths provided. One of the cloths will be intended for polishing the instrument (usually blue). The other will be intended for use with the cleaning rod, to clear away moisture from the inside of the instrument. If this is cotton then it should work well, but sometimes a synthetic or felt cloth is provided, in which case you would do better to use a square of soft cotton which will be more absorbent – a man sized handkerchief works well.

Thread the corner of your cloth through the eye of the cleaning rod. To clean away the moisture in the foot joint and body of the flute you can simply push the rod and cloth through one side and out the other. With the head joint, push gently forwards and back a couple of times.

Be careful not to push against the resistance of the crown. If you dislodge this, it will alter the tuning.

Packing the flute in its case after each playing session will keep it protected from dust and dirt. Leaving the lid of the case open for ten minutes before closing it will enable the flute to dry out thoroughly.

Try to store the cleaning rod and cloth separate from the flute if you can. Moisture from the cloth will then be kept away from the flute.

Cleaning the outside:

The polishing cloth can be used to wipe away moisture and grease marks from contact areas – the lip plate and all the keys where the fingers have been placed in playing or holding the flute. Use a gentle circular motion. It is a good idea to do this at the end of each playing session. There is a certain amount of acidity in the sweat produced by the body, and this can eat away at the metal coating.

Acid on the fingers

Do not be tempted to use a silver cloth or any product for polishing the metal. Most flutes are silver-plated, and the quality and thickness of the plating varies, depending on make and model. It's a question of maintaining the appearance of your flute whilst being careful not to wear away the plating.

Another temptation is to feed the cloth between the keys to clear away any dust. If you do this you are likely to do more damage than good. Key work and springs can get bent or dislodged and the delicate pads can get damaged.

Avoiding stiff joints:

Finish up by polishing the tenons, where metal touches metal when you put the sections together. Moisture and dust can quickly settle here and create a build-up of gunge. This prevents things sliding together easily.

If this happens, use a small amount of lighter fluid on a separate cloth, and rub the tenon clean, firmly but gently. Using any kind of grease lubricant will make things easier initially, but it acts as a magnet for dust and dirt. This makes for more of a problem in the long run.

The Crown:

This is the section that stops one end of the head joint. It is advisable to leave this well alone. Screwing it either way will affect the length of tube inside the head-joint, and this will affect the tuning between the registers.

You can check if this is correctly positioned by sliding your cleaning rod into the head-joint, eye end first. The groove in the cleaning rod should appear exactly halfway along the embouchure hole.

Correct position of the crown - cleaning rod notch should be half way along embouchure hole

If this is off centre, then best take the flute to your technician or a teacher who can re-adjust this for you.

23

TROUBLE SHOOTING AND MAINTENANCE.

If you clean your flute through thoroughly after playing, there should be few issues. However, here are some that students have experienced.

Notes not speaking or sounding weak

1. One or more of the pads is not seated correctly over the hole.

2. A pad is split and needs replacing

3. A key is bent

4. One or more balancing screws need re-adjusting. *(Balancing screws are the very tiny screws located above some of the keys – they regulate the distance between the pads and the holes on which they seat.)*

In all of these cases, take your flute to a technician. An experienced flautist will carry a tiny screwdriver and know how to tweak the screw adjustments. Sometimes a tiny tweak will do the trick, but unless you thoroughly understand the mechanism, you could throw other keys out of adjustment and compound the problem.

Problems sliding the sections together

Common problems:

1. Dust and moisture collecting between the joints. This can be avoided if you clean the joints after playing (see Chapter 22). If, despite cleaning, the problem persists, then it will need attention from your technician.

2. One of the tenons could be slightly bent. Take it to your technician,

Sticky Pads:

Use cigarette papers: place one sheet between the pad and the hole it covers. Press down gently on the metal cup holding the pad and then release. Repeat this action until the cigarette paper appears dry. Do not pull the paper whilst pressing down. Flute pads have a double skin that is particularly delicate. If you do this you may tear the pad, or you may tear the paper, leaving parts of it in the flute body.

If the stickiness persists, then you can purchase powder paper from a woodwind shop. Ensure the pad is dry by using the cigarette paper first, then use the powder paper. This will leave a slight residue of powder on the pad and prevent it sticking.

NB

If you avoid eating or drinking before playing, then you will rarely have this problem! No sticky breath - cleaner pads.

Feasting before you play leads to sticky pads

Servicing

As with a car, your flute will need to be serviced from time to time. How much you play will determine the regularity of this, (just as how many miles you drive determines the regularity of your car service). You can take your flute to be serviced every six months, every year or two years.

A full service will require taking all the keys off the flute and a thorough technician will normally clean up any extra debris and give the body a polish.

The technician will check the springs have the correct tension to hold the keys up or down, and that the tiny adjustment screws are correctly balanced so the pads seal correctly on the holes.

The pads themselves will also be checked to ensure that they are in good order, creating an airtight seal when in place.

Finally, the mechanism will be lubricated to ensure ease of movement throughout.

Keep your flute in tip-top condition, and it will serve you well.

24

ACCESSORIES

Music Stand

Always use a music stand. It will improve your posture, and prevent you straining your neck while trying to read at an angle. The collapsible type is great for getting out and about and playing with other musicians.

Flute Stand

This can be useful. Ideally, the flute should be kept in its case between playing sessions (see Chapter 22), but if you are just taking a short break, a stand will prevent the instrument from getting knocked or damaged and keep the flow of moisture from collecting under the pads.

Cleaning Rod

A wooden rod is preferable to a metal rod because it will not scratch the inside of the tube. Use it with a cotton cloth that is large enough to clean the tube thoroughly, but not so large that you have to force it through.

Extra Anchorage

The flute can feel slippery and difficulty to manage in the early stages of learning, particularly when moving between lower and upper registers across C, C$^{\#}$ and D. If your posture and hand positions are correct, you should soon feel sufficiently secure (see chapter 5). However, if you feel some extra support would motivate you to play more regularly, it is worth considering the following:

Left-finger rest. This clips on the head-joint and helps to prevent the head-joint slipping and rolling.

Right-thumb finger rest. This clips on the body of the flute. Clip it just where the right thumb should be placed, adjusting with correct anchorage in mind (see chapter 4),and it should help prevent the body of the flute rolling inwards.

25

BACK PAGE

READING FROM THE END BACKWARDS

It is an odd fact that mistakes often happen towards the end of a piece of music. Here are some possible reasons why.

Typical practice habit

Most people start at the beginning (an obvious place to start). They go wrong, start again, go wrong, start again, etc, etc, etc.

The end of the piece rarely gets played

The beginning gets played many times, but the end of the piece rarely gets reached—so that section doesn't get played very often - it's not very familiar.

Concentration diminishes

Most people are more alert at the beginning of a task. We take for granted the simultaneous skill of reading music with the coordination involved in playing an instrument. This requires a huge amount of concentration.

Anxiety increases

As you venture into uncharted territory, the likelihood of going wrong is greater.

Solution:

Start your practice session with the end of the piece.

Persistence of practice has always been the case...

From Dickens Old Curiosity Shop

Mr. Swiveller playing the Flute -- the fifty-seventh illustration for the novel in Master Humphrey's Clock, *Part 35. 3 **4 % inches (8.9 cm high x 11 cm wide Charles Dickens's Old Curiosity Shop, Part 32 (London: Chapman & Hall, 12 December 1840). Chapter 58, 124*

Passage Illustrated: The Melancholy Musician – A Romantic Pose

Some men in his blighted position would have taken to drinking: but as Mr. Swiveller had taken to that before. he only took, on receiving the news that Sophy Wacktes was lost to him for over, to playing the flute; thinking after mature consideration that it was a good, sound. dismal occupation, not only in unison with his own sad thoughts, but calculated to awaken a fellow-feeling in the bosoms of his neighbours. In pursuance of this resolution, he now drew a little table to his bedside, and arranging the light and a small oblong music-book to the best advantage, took his flute from its box, and began to play most mournfully ...The air was "Away with Melancholy" a composition, which, when it is played very slowly on the flute, in bed, with the further disadvantage of being performed by a gentleman but imperfectly acquainted with the instrument, who repeats one note a great many times before he can find the next, has not a lively effect. Yet, for half the night or more, Mr Swiveller, lying sometimes on his back with his eyes upon the ceiling, and sometimes half out of bed to correct himself by the book, played this unhappy tune over and over again: never leaving off, save for a minute or two at a time to take breath and soliloquise about the Marchioness, and then beginning again with a new vigour. It was not until he had quite exhausted his several subjects of meditation, and had breathed into the flute the whole sentiment of the purl down to its very dregs, and had nearly maddened the people of the house, and at both the next doors, and over the way - that he shut up the music book, extinguished the candle, and finding himself greatly lightened and relieved in his mind, turned round and fell asleep. (Chapter the 58th. 124)

ABOUT THE AUTHOR

Louise graduated from the London College of Music with ALCM and LLCM and began her first post as Woodwind teacher for North Devon LEA. Since her subsequent post as Woodwind tutor for Blundell's School, Louise's ongoing freelance work in Somerset has involved teaching people of all ages and performing with a variety of Classical, Jazz and Klezmer ensembles.

Her music projects have been many and varied. They include co-founding *The High Park Community Music School,* which enables any child to play music; forming the adult band *Hoot* moving adults towards improvisation; and collaborating on *The Mosaic of Art and Vision,* workshops designed to teach children how to create art inspired by music.

Since gaining a B Sc (Hons) in Psychology, Louise has focussed attention on the hurdles that limit playing potential and developing *Wizwind.* This innovative and compelling teaching method is designed for people who struggle to read music, enabling students to choose a tune one week and be playing it the next. The *Wizwind* method liberates students whose reliance on reading music prevents them from developing their improvising potential.

During Covid, when restrictions have allowed, fellow musicians have trekked to rehearse in a large barn where Louise lives on a remote farm, warmed by a fire pit and overlooking fields of bemused cattle.

The Self Taught Flute Player was inspired by a realisation that not everyone is so lucky. Some insights from a friendly musician who has 'done her time in the cells' (as music students term it) might encourage and spur on the lonely blower at this challenging time.

Look out for further Wizwind inspirations coming your way soon!

Printed in Great Britain
by Amazon

57882752R00056